THIS BOOK IS THE PROPERTY OF

LUTHER TARBOX

by Jan Adkins

CHARLES SCRIBNER'S SONS · NEW YORK

Copyright © 1977 Jan Adkins

Library of Congress Cataloging in Publication Data

Adkins, Jan.

Luther Tarbox.

SUMMARY: A lobsterman out in his boat in a heavy
fog is approached by sailors, on varying sizes of
boats and ships, seeking guidance into port.

[1. Boats and boating—Fiction. 2. Ships—Fiction]
I. Title.

PZ7.A2612Lu   [E]   77-6711

ISBN 0-684-14931-1

1 3 5 7 9 11 13 15 17 19 MD/C 20 18 16 14 12 10 8 6 4 2

Printed in the United States of America

Set in a Linofilm Baskerville with Morgan Press wooden display faces.

for Debo; so long, pal

Luther Tarbox was a lucky man. In all his lucky life, four things made him happiest:

His wife, Jessie, who was a friend and partner and sweetheart all in one strong woman. She knew the water as well as Luther did, she wove strong nets, she made the best chowder on Buzzards Bay, and she made him very happy. When he was pulling his lobster pots in the fog or way off on the Weepecket Rocks he thought about her.

He had a boat, the *Sylvia B.*, a broad-beamed, bold-bowed catboat with one mast like a polished telephone pole and a sail big enough to cover a barn. She would work a hard-jawed way up into the wind if you asked her, but with the wind behind her she was as light and quick as a doe on a meadow.

Luther had a brass-bound, oil-filled compass on double gimbals in a rosewood box. It was a true and unswerving friend, pointing toward magnetic north as surely as the North Star points true north, and when night came or the weather sponged out the sight of land, it made him very happy.

Luther was lucky to have something *in* him that made him happy every day. He had a pure tenor voice as clear and sweet as spring water. He sang lively in the morning —"Paddy West" or "The House Carpenter"— and when the packet boat *Alert* passed him in the afternoon, Captain Ludgero Gomes (who had a bass voice like chocolate sauce poured over fudge-nut brownies) rang down to the engine room for "both engines stop" so he could sing at least one verse of "Rolling Home" with Luther. And in the evening...ah, in the evening...Luther Tarbox would ghost into harbor with the sunset and the last bit of breeze, singing "Shenandoah" so high and fine that folks ashore stopped their cooking and put down their papers and just listened. You would, too. He was a lucky man.

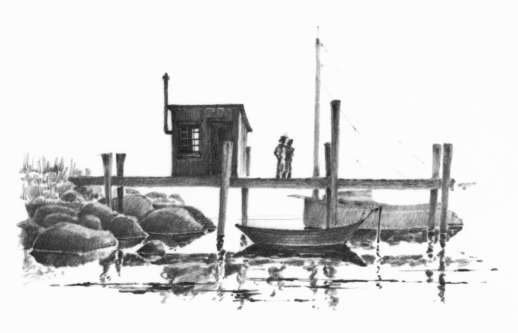

There was a morning in June that began quiet but damp. Drops of water hung on the screens and beaded on the tips of the grass. Jessie stoked a fire to chase the damp out of her kitchen.

"Damp day," she said over the cod cakes.

Luther poured their tea. "Smoky sou'wester," he replied, and when they walked down to the dock with his gear the bay was dim in the smoke-white haze of the moist breeze.

"Fog?" she asked.

"Maybe," he said, and opened his compass.

They stacked his lobster pots in the *Sylvia B*'s cockpit, hefted the bait barrel aboard and, after Jessie gave his cheek a pat, she cast off the docking lines.

He drifted out past the dory stake and Jessie called after him, "Chowder tonight." It was not too far away to see him smile. Then he bent to the halyards and hoisted the sail, and the *Sylvia B.* slid away. Walking back up the path, she could hear him begin singing:

As I went walking on Main Royal Street
I came to Paddy West's house,
He gave me a bowl of American hash
And he called it Liverpool scouse.

Sure enough, while Luther was eating his lunch, a fog bank rolled over Buzzards Bay, white and dense as the inside of a cotton ball. He finished up his sandwich and started in to work again, pulling up pots and taking the keepers. He threw back the small lobsters and the lobsters carrying eggs under their tails; he rebaited the pots with codheads and flounderbacks and dumped them over the side. From one buoy to the next he worked, watching his sail and his compass, and singing:

In this windy old weather
Stormy old weather, boys,
When the winds blow
We'll all go together.

He finished one verse and was about to begin another when a voice came out of the fog: "Hello, hello! Hello, over there! Don't go, for mercy sakes!" A rowboat followed the voice out of the fog and drifted with a thump right into the *Sylvia B.*

"Good grief, captain! I have been rowing in this unwholesome fog for an hour and three-quarters. At long last I heard your singing and I said to Samson here, 'A man who can sing in this fog is a man who knows where he is,' and we rowed right toward the sound. So, captain, where are we?"

Luther looked at the woman and her dog for a moment and said, "You're lost."

"Well, I couldn't agree with you more, captain. Just point the way home and we'll be off."

Luther shook his head. "You'd be lost again. Hang on to the stern here while I pull my pots, and I'll take you in."

"Why, that would be real nice." She sat down with her dog as Luther made her bow line fast to a cleat. "You just go ahead with your work, now."

Luther smiled and turned to his pots and his boat and his song:

Up spoke the crab
With his great claws,
He cried out, O captain,
Come haul through the hawse,
In this windy old weather,
Stormy old weather, boys,
When the winds blow
We'll all go together.

A few pots and a few verses later he heard a noise, a buzz like a hoarse mosquito changing direction back and forth in the fog. He sang on. The woman in the boat was beginning to sing with him on the choruses. The buzz grew louder and hoarser until a motorboat shot into view and out of sight again. It circled in the fog while the rowboat and the *Sylvia B.* bobbed and rolled in its wake, and then it purred back with its motor idling.

"Hiyah, fellah. Hiyah, lady," said the man behind the steering wheel. "We got us a little fog here. Which way to the fish dock?"

"Do you have a good compass and a chart aboard?" asked Luther.

The man shifted his cigar from one side of his mouth to the other. "Never carry 'em," he said.

"I do," said Luther, "and I can take you in, but I've got to pull my pots first."

The man shifted his cigar again and looked around at the fog. "Right," he said, and pushed his levers into reverse to back the motorboat into line behind the rowboat. "I'm with ya."

Luther glanced at his compass, hauled at the mainsheet, and sailed off toward the next pot, singing:

Up spoke the mack'rel
With his stripèd back
He cried out, O skipper,
Come on your port tack
In this windy old weather,
Stormy old weather, boys...

Now there was another sound in the fog, a strangled sort of moo. Luther heard the motorboatman ask, "Is there a cow out here?" but he went on singing until a white shape broke out of the fog just ahead.

"Hard-a-port!" called Luther and turned the wheel. The *Sylvia B.* and the rowboat and the motorboat turned to the left as a small sailboat hissed through the water on their right. A long-haired girl was at the tiller and a surprised young man held a foghorn to his mouth. Their blocks creaked and their sails flapped as they spun their little daysailer around and brought it up off the *Sylvia B.*'s stern.

The young man said, "Ah, ahhh, we're, uh…"

"Lost in the bloody fog," said the girl.

Luther nodded, "Yes, you are," he said.

"I wonder if you might, er, ah, we need, ahh…"

"Sit down, Donald," the girl said. "This bloody compass is at least twenty degrees off, and a fog like this is no place to correct it."

"I wonder, er, we wonder, that is…"

"Be quiet, Donald."

"I've got to pull my pots first, but afterwards…" Luther began.

"Right," she said, throwing her tiller over and sheeting in the sails. "We'll follow you in." The little boat spun around and fell into line behind the motorboat.

"Hiyah, sis," said the motorboatman.

"Watch your steering," she said, and they steered behind the *Sylvia B.* as it headed for the next buoy, Luther singing:

Up spoke the sprat,
The smallest of all,
He cried out, O captain,
Come haul your trail haul
In this windy old weather,
Stormy old weather, boys...

"Rum bum plum dumb numb sum…" came a murmur in the fog.

"Well, *something* is out there, Samson," said the woman in the rowboat. "Yoo hoo! Captain, something is out there in the fog."

Luther smiled and nodded, singing, and before he could finish another verse, a grey motorcruiser murmured into view. Its owner stepped onto the stern deck with a teacup in one hand and a saucer in the other.

"Hello, my good man. Heard your song out there. Delightful, just delightful. Substantial weather we're having, isn't it?"

"Your boat is sitting on my number eight pot," Luther said.

"Ah, yes, a day of some proportions. Say there, sailor, I'll bet you could give my captain the bearing into the yacht club."

"Lost?" asked Luther.

"I wouldn't go so far as to say that, exactly," the owner said, examining the rim of his teacup. "Rather, I would say, perhaps, that we are…"

"Lost in the bloody fog," called the girl from the daysailer.

The owner looked up with a strained smile. "Yes," he said.

"First off," said Luther, "move that boat off my number eight pot. Then fall into line and I'll take you in."

"After the pots are pulled," said the woman in the rowboat.

Luther pulled number eight with the boats strung out behind him, singing (with harmony on the chorus now):

Up spoke the finback
With his great black tail,
He cried out, O skipper,
Come reef in your sail
In this windy old weather,
Stormy old weather, boys…

By now it was no surprise to hear the rumble of big diesel engines in the fog ahead. Before long the steel bow of the Coast Guard launch *Observant* sliced through the fog and stopped beside the *Sylvia B.* A young man in uniform walked out onto the foredeck and called down, "Captain Tarbox? Is that you, sir?"

"Is that Teddy O'Leary up there?" Luther replied.

"Yes, sir. Yes sir, it's Lieutenant O'Leary, here."

"Where is Charlie Johnson?"

"Seaman Johnson is belowdecks trying to repair our radar and our radio direction finder, sir, and I expect a restoration of service momentarily."

"Charlie," Luther called, "how's it coming along down there?"

Seaman Johnson rose slowly out of the radio room hatch, shook his head sadly, and disappeared again.

"If you could give us our position, sir, I'm sure we could make our way back to the Coast Guard station."

"Teddy, you take your launch back to the end of the line, and as soon as I pull a few more pots I'll take you in."

"Thank you, sir, but where is the end of the line?"

"Back there in the fog, just behind the gray motorcruiser, son."

Luther hauled in the sail, the wind filled it, and the *Sylvia B.* moved on with its floating parade behind it, Seaman Johnson's fine baritone joining the chorus:

Up spoke the herring,
The king of the sea,
He cried out, O skipper,
Oh, you can't catch me
In this windy old weather,
Stormy old weather, boys...

When the *Sylvia B.* glided up to a buoy off Cleveland Ledge, someone was waiting. Fifteen feet above the buoy hung a golden eagle, and above the eagle—on a varnished bowsprit—sat Captain Douglas of the topsail schooner *Shenandoah.*

"Hello there, Captain Tarbox," said Captain Douglas.

"Hello, yourself," said Luther.

"Heard you singing. Need a job of piloting us in through this fog."

"Glad to help," said Luther.

"Is that my wife's aunt you've got hanging off your stern?" Captain Douglas asked, staring at the woman in the rowboat.

"Wouldn't know."

"Aunt Maisie," shouted Captain Douglas, "is that you?"

"Hello, Bobby. Say hello, Samson."

"Luther, half of Massachusetts must be following you."

"And some of Rhode Island!" came a voice out of the fog.

"Well, lead on," Captain Douglas said.

"I've got just a few more pots," Luther replied, and bent to his work.

Up spoke the bluefish
With his toothy mouth,
He cried out, O captain,
Come steer East by South
In this windy old weather,
Stormy old weather, boys,
When the wind blows
We'll all go together!

Jessie Tarbox had finished her chowder—enough chowder to last for two weeks —and now she stood in the doorway mending nets, listening. She thought she heard...or did she, so faint and far? Again, yes, it was Luther, now she could hear him clearly, but she could also hear a dozen other voices singing with him. She walked down to the dock to see what would come out of the fogbank. She smiled as Luther and the *Sylvia B.* emerged, she laughed at the rowboat that followed and laughed more at the motorboat, the daysailer, the cabin cruiser, the Coast Guard launch, and even the 104-foot schooner *Shenandoah.*

But when the ponderous black bow of the Japanese oil tanker *Tokyo Maru* broke out of the fog, 70 feet high and almost as wide as the cove, Jessie had to sit down on a piling head.

That night they all had the best fish chowder on Buzzards Bay, and they were almost as happy as Luther. Almost, but not quite, because Luther Tarbox was a lucky man.